my brother's gun

my brother's gun

ray loriga

translated by
kristina cordero

st. martin's press
new york

Book design by Scott Levine

Library of Congress Cataloging-in-Publication Data

Loriga, Ray,
    [Caídos del cielo. English]
    My brother's gun / Ray Loriga; translated by Kristina Cordero.
        p.   cm.
    ISBN 0–312–16947–7
    I. Cordero, Kristina.   II. Title.
    PQ6662.O77C3513   1997
    863' .64—dc21   97–16233

Originally published in Spanish as *Caídos del cielo* by Plaza & Janés Editores, S.A. Copyright © 1995 by Ray Loriga.

First U.S. edition: September 1997
10   9   8   7   6   5   4   3   2   1

i'd rather be thin than famous.

—jack kerouac

part of Beat
Generation
in 50s

- escape
- moving away from society
- rejection of mainstream
- experiments w/ sex + drugs
- interest in eastern spirituality

leave the kids alone

pinkfloyd - "the wall"

"So?"

He didn't really know what he was asking. All morning his stomach had been killing him. Really killing him. A sharp pain, like a nail. I know, because she told me herself, before she told me about the gun. The gun wasn't hers. That's what they had said, but it wasn't true. The gun was his, all right. They came up with a lot of bullshit, but anyway, it was his. For sure. A big black automatic gun.

"He's not moving."
"He won't. He's dead. Like me."
"You're not dead."
"I will be."

He had a point. Two hours later, they filled him with bullets; so many that you wouldn't have recognized him. You would have had to really love him to be able to look at him like that. That's how bad it was. My mother didn't go. Nobody really loved him, anyway. Nobody at all.

She didn't. I think she had seen too many movies. She was kind of out of touch. But there's a fine line between that and love.

"It's not that gross."

"No."

"Or even all that sad."

"It is what it is. Let's get out of here."

He got into the car. He remembered our mother, I'm sure he remembered our mother saying, "Something tells me this is all going to seem better in the morning." He started the car and said:

"Something tells me this isn't going to seem better in the morning."

2

When anybody, like the TV people for example, asks me about him, I always say that I don't think it was such a good idea what he did. Because it's the truth, and anyway, my mother would die if I said anything else. But, to tell you the real truth, he wasn't such a bad guy. Besides, what the fuck, he was my brother. TV reporters, they're such assholes. I mean, the questions they ask, like, did he ever aim a gun at me? My own brother?! Are you kidding? Yeah, with his aim, yeah, I probably *would* be dead by now. Dead like our old dog Dark. We called him Dark after the movie *Darkman*. You know, the one where the guy changes his face all the time and turns into everything, anything. My brother loved both the movie and the dog. A truck ran over Dark.

"All right. You can come with me, but I'm telling you it's a mistake."

"How would you know?"

"I know."

They were silent for a while after that. He drove really fast, enough to scare you. Good and fast. Then she started talking. She talked a lot.

"God only knows how many good things are still to come."

He cut her off.

"Do you love me?"

"What?"

He repeated what he had just said.

"Sure I do, of course I do . . . so, do you want me to suck you off?"

"You suck everyone off."

"Yeah, and you go around killing people, which is worse."

"No shit."

They didn't say anything else after that for a while.

Thirty miles later, he stopped, opened the door, and kicked her out. He wasn't going that fast, though. I mean, he never hurt a girl on purpose. Much less her. I think he even liked her a little.

The first thing that I should say here is my brother was *not* a fag. A virgin, yeah, but not a fag. Or maybe he was; I don't really know for sure. That's not the point. The point is, those fucking TV reporters said he was a fag right from the beginning, and they didn't even know him. It was all because of something she had said, and she didn't even mean it that way. Those fucking TV people, they think that because they never killed anybody they're perfect or something, but they're wrong. I can tell you, those guys are the biggest assholes I've ever seen in my whole entire life.

Before, I used to like TV. Now I can't stand to even look at a television set.

For my own part, I should admit that I'm a virgin too. But I'm definitely not a fag. One has nothing to do with the other. It's not that I don't want to do it, I just never had the chance.

It was only three days before he shot the guy at the gas station that she had insisted on staying in the car and going with him, everywhere. She also wanted him to fuck her. They were in the backseat:

"Why don't you fuck me?"

She loved saying things like that.

"Not here. It's too cramped."

"Come on, what are you talking about? There's more than enough room."

"This is where we're *sleeping*."

They slept there because they weren't old enough to stay at a hotel. Maybe she could've. But he looked young for his age.

"Everybody fucks in the same place they sleep."

"Well, I'm not everybody."

That was how he dealt with things when they started getting out of hand. After that, there was nothing. End of story.

He talked like they do in the movies, and he didn't even *go* to the movies all that much. That was another thing. The TV reporters made him out to be some sort of TV freak. They would show short movie clips and then say he was trying to be just like *them.* Sorry, guys. Wrong again. My brother was not one of those kooks who imitate what they see in the movies. My brother had a gun, and he killed two guys who probably deserved what they got, anyway. Sure, so he was a little off. I'm not denying that. But a freak? No way.

I tried explaining all of this to my mother, but, incredibly, she preferred to believe what they were saying on TV. I couldn't believe it. His own mother! She was impossible. You couldn't talk to her at all. But I guess that's what happens. When people saw her on the street, they'd say, "Look, that's the Angel of Death's mother." That's what the TV people called him, because he was so fucking good-looking. When they showed his photo in the newspaper, the girls all went crazy, writing letters, tons and tons of letters. I still have them. Love letters, that sort of thing. He even got a few letters from guys, real psychos. Those I threw out.

He never knew about all this. He was already dead when the letters started coming.

They're still writing to him. It's like writing to a ghost. They tell him everything.

They also write to her. That's what she told me.

She wanted to be a singer.

"What's in those little bags?"

"Beans."

"Beans?"

"Yes, it's good exercise. I put a pound of them on my stomach, and then I flex my muscles. It helps my flow of oxygen, you know. It gives me a broader vocal range. It's a respiratory thing. You sing from your stomach, you know."

"Beans for singing? I've never heard of that before."

"There's lots of things you've never heard of, killer. Fucking, for example. I bet you don't even know what it is."

"How about, for example, shooting a girl point-blank. I haven't done that either, but that doesn't mean I wouldn't."

The truth is, he didn't like people messing with him like that.

I guess that scared her pretty bad. She told me she thought it was funny, but I'm pretty sure he scared her.

Sometimes, not always.

3

We used to spend summers at the beach. He hated it. Not the water; he didn't hate the water at all. He loved to stare out at the water, and then go in alone, after it was already dark. It was the beach he hated. The guys all cruising for girls. The whole concept of the beach drove him nuts. I don't know if "concept" is the right word, but you know what I mean. They can say whatever they want on TV, but I can tell you my brother did not like guys. He hated everything guys are supposed to naturally love, like bicycles, windsurfing, big tits, and the beach. He never wanted to jump down from anything, or climb up to the top of anything. He just wanted to be left alone. So maybe he was a fag after all. What do I know, I mean, what am I, an expert or something? I get along okay with fags. They seem all right to me, but then again, everybody usually seems all right to me.

Not to my brother.

"Are you going to just do nothing all day?"

"Leave me alone. What do you want me to do? I'm lying

on the beach. That's what I'm doing. Lying on the beach. What are *you* doing that's so important?"

"Reading."

"Big deal."

I was only a kid then. Now I read a lot.

"You don't know it yet, but reading's the best. TV and movies are okay, too. I mean, you know how I feel about *Terminator.* The first one, though—the second one was shit. Reading is different, and then it's not so different, all at the same time."

It drove me nuts when he'd get all logical like that, because I never knew what he was talking about. I'd rather see him kill people than get all logical like that.

"Read whatever you want, I don't care. I'm going to swim out to the buoys."

I always wanted to swim out to the buoys, but I never made it all the way out there. The angrier I got at him, the more I wanted to reach those buoys, but I'd always get wiped out halfway.

He would go out to the buoys, and then swim back, like it was nothing. He did it when he thought no one was watching.

The buoys were far off.

4

Blood is disgusting. Everyone thinks so, I mean, it's not some big revelation.

My mother kept saying this.

"I don't know how he stands the sight of blood."

She said, "I don't know how he *stands,*" but she should have said *"stood,"* because when they showed her the photos, he was already dead. In another photo . . . but they didn't show her that one.

"Those poor people. What a shame."

We were at the police station, and she was looking at the photos. The cops brought out about a thousand Polaroids of the two people he killed, as if to say: *See, we had no other choice.*

My mother examined the photos closely, turning them this way and that. Like those abstract pictures you never know which way to hang. My brother shot one guy in the face. At first, I refused to look at the photos, but then I changed my mind. They were pretty gross, and it was hard to believe that he actually had something to do with all of it. He was so fucking good-looking.

It's not like I have anything against abstract art. Really. I love it. The truth is, I can't stand realism. In school they took us to an Antonio López exhibition and I almost died. I had never seen anything uglier in my whole life. I know that art experts always say there's no such thing as ugly, but this was ugly. I swear. Ugly as hell.

My mother was talking to herself.

"Those clothes he was wearing . . ."

My mother seems to think there's a direct relationship between wearing ripped jeans and killing people.

The cops kept shoving photos in her face. They acted like they were all sympathetic, but I know they kind of thought it was her fault too. That we were all at fault.

There was one cop, by the door, who looked like a nice guy. He was the only one in a uniform.

"It's that these kids, they don't even have a father . . ."

He said that father thing while staring straight at me. As if to say, *This one's next. If you want, we can kill him right now and wrap this whole case up.*

If there's anything that makes me sick it's this whole father thing. I know about a million jerks who have fathers. People just say things like that without even thinking. As if that explained anything. You don't have a father, so you're a killer. Like, you live in a brick house, so you're a fireman.

Brilliant reasoning on the part of the police.

More photos. They were driving my poor mother insane.

"Look at these, ma'am. Shot right in the face, a family man. It's a real tragedy we've got here."

"I know that, young man, of course it is."

She didn't know what she was saying; the cop was at least ten years older than her.

My mother is very young. And very beautiful, too.

"We better keep an eye on this one."

I was sitting in the corner, not saying anything. I slid off the fake leather chair and just about fell on the floor, but I wasn't about to open my mouth, not for anything.

It was like there were two cats in the house, and one had just finished off the canary. I was the second cat.

The world is full of canaries.

5

"Maybe I'll shoot you."

He had barely said it when he'd blown the security guard's cap off his head. Only one shot, the first one. Almost by accident.

The guard fell backward, his face full of smoke. After that, he didn't move much.

I don't know if you've ever been in one of those places

where you can buy just about anything: magazines, alcohol, flowers, canned soup, videotapes, and then top it all off with a milk shake. But that's not the point. The point is, the guards at those places are the biggest fucking assholes in the world.

It goes something like this. You go in, you buy something, and they give you a receipt. You go into the cafeteria section for a drink, then you lose the receipt. When you try to leave the place, the guard stops you, and he asks for the receipt. If you don't have it, he grabs you, and then you look at him like you could kill him, right there.

He added something to it.

You pull out a gun. A gun that's black as hell, and you blow his head off.

6

The best of all was the way he drove. Nobody could drive like him. He was the only person I ever knew who learned to drive on his first try. He'd spin a car around, just like in the movies. It was like he had driving in his blood, although

I know he didn't. It hadn't been in his blood at all because my mother's a miserable driver. It seemed he always instinctively knew exactly what a car was going to do. Even when it had looked like he was going to crash. He never crashed. Not even once. Because of that, you would always feel safer with him than with anyone else.

"Just wait for this next curve," he'd say.

My stomach would already be in my ears when he'd suddenly slam on the brakes, and then approach the curve like he was surfing a wave.

For a second we were on two wheels.

"God, did you see that? Did you see that, shrimp?"

Shrimp was what he always called me. I didn't find it funny at all, but that's what he used to call me. It wasn't because of my height. I was two years younger, but I was almost as tall as him.

My mother's car slowed down until it finally came to a full stop, exactly in front of the record store. He'd promised to take me shopping for records that day. And there we were.

"Don't be afraid, it was nothing."

That was so typical of him. He'd scare the hell out of you first, then he'd try to make you feel better.

We went into the record store and they had all the records, even some old ones that we'd been trying to find for a while. They were all there. When it came to music, we liked exactly the same things. He knew more about music than I did, but if I discovered a new band, he'd love them, too.

We were broke that day, so we only got the latest Nirvana CD. A few days after that, Kurt Cobain was dead. Ten days later, so was my brother. That's why they insisted on bringing Cobain into the picture, when the truth is, the one thing had nothing to do with the other.

You should have heard the kind of shit they were asking me. I can't believe they'd say things like that to me: "Your brother, the murderer," like it was no big deal. As if you could hear that and just deal with it.

"Cold-blooded Murder, Committed by an Angel of Death." And all because he was so fucking good-looking. It really pissed them off that he was so good-looking. He was a monster, and monsters were supposed to be ugly. That's how they saw things, I guess.

One thing I never told them: "Ladies and gentlemen of the press, go fuck yourselves."

The day we found out about Cobain, three days after he shot himself in the mouth, my brother said to me: "There are so many ways to ruin a good guy. Sometimes you can see it coming, and sometimes you can't."

7

"Bet you can't jump the fence."

"Yeah. I bet I can't." My brother was a genius at avoiding dares.

"Why don't the two of you just get the fuck out of here?"

A kid had grabbed a stick and was shaking it at me, to scare me, like the way you scare a dog.

My brother pounced on him so fast he didn't even see it coming. They started rolling around on the ground until the other kid began making these noises, like he was being strangled. The truth is, he was being strangled. When the teachers broke them up, my brother looked over at me, satisfied, and I was too. I always knew that no matter what, I could count on him. And then all those people came here, to my house, with their big mouths, pointing their big fingers at me, thinking I'm going to help them? No way, man.

I mean, I did all I could for my poor mother, she was such a wreck. But through the whole thing, no one could ever say that I ever once bad-mouthed my brother.

They gave my mother and me almost a whole half hour on the weekly news. My mother looked beautiful, like a movie star. I wore my brother's leather jacket, even though it was a little big on me. We were seated on a stage, in front of a group of people, who clapped for us when we first came out. They kept clapping, it seemed, every time my mother or I or the interviewer said anything in a loud enough voice.

"How do we know that the Angel of Death's *brother* isn't a monster as well?"

Applause.

My mother looked at me, waiting for me to answer the question. Then the camera zoomed in on me.

I didn't say anything.

8

There was a lot more to see. The mountain behind the dunes, and then the sea.

"If you don't come up here, you're nothing; if you don't make it to the top, you're nowhere; if you chicken out, you die; and if you fall, you're lost."

.   .   .

He was happy. She told me. She said, "Nobody had probably ever seen him as happy as he was right then."

He was wearing his leather boots, even though it was hard to walk through the sand in them. She had a pair of cut-offs on and a tiny blue stretch T-shirt. To tell the truth, she was great-looking too. Red hair, long legs. He was a little shorter than her.

She had small tits. She still has them. Like a little girl. She told me about them over the phone, and then I saw them myself. She showed them to me.

I can't tell now if she ever really loved him, or if she was only following him because he was so good-looking or because he drove like a psycho or because he killed people. I don't know.

There were a lot of things he could do that nobody else did. But I guess there are a lot of things everyone else does that he was totally unable to do.

He kept climbing the dune that day, and the sea was bigger than anything else. He loved the sea. It was the beach he hated. He loved the water and he loved the sand. He just didn't like all those people there.

He did like nice people. The reporters got that wrong, too. He was crazy about really nice people, he could spend hours and hours talking to nice people he didn't even know. Hours and hours. He never even talked to me for hours and hours.

Then they went around saying he was an introverted sociopath, a loner. But I'm getting used to that.

.   .   .

He slid down the dune until he reached the water. He went in with his boots on. It was hot as hell, but he always wore his boots. He was standing in the water up to his waist when a wave crashed over him. He was wearing his black jeans, a black V-necked T-shirt, and his leather boots.

Nobody had ever seen him looking as amazing as he did then.

That's what she told me.

"You'll never dry off," she said to him.

"I don't want to dry off. I want to drown. And you can't be dry when you drown. You've got to be soaking wet."

She admitted to me that she never knew if she really loved him, but right then she did. Of course, the day he kicked her out of the car, she stopped loving him forever.

When she reached the bottom of the dune, she saw the mountain. Then she saw him in the water. And it was at that moment—and she still swears it—when she knew that nobody had ever seen him look so incredible.

They were lying down in the sand.

"I didn't know you were such a good swimmer. You've got a strange body."

"What do you mean, strange?"

"I don't know . . . Well, like a tired athlete or . . . an energetic bum."

"Well, that's exactly how I want to look."

He was so fucking proud of it.

She really didn't love him that much. I mean, she wouldn't have risked her life for him or anything, but she probably had flashes like that, when she truly thought she'd never seen a guy like him in the whole world.

They began eating. They brought ham and cheese and

bread and six beers. He got out of the water, went all the way up to the car, and brought everything down to her. Twice he went up and down the dune. She was tired.

She was good-looking, too. First she told me on the phone, and then finally I saw her for myself, or maybe I knew it before she told me. She said: "I'm pretty; that's why he took me with him." I don't think she's a bad person—she's just a little crazy, that's all. After what happened, all the letters she got, plus the TV and the photos and everything else, it fucked her up. And now that it's all over, she acts like a star, or maybe she really *is* a star. Well, at least, she looks like one.

I don't know. Everything that happened afterward was so bizarre that I guess we all just did whatever we could.

"What are you going to do now?" she asked him.

He was still lying in the sand. He didn't want to do anything.

"Dry off."

Because he had shot that security guard, a guy with a first name and a last name, with children and a wife and a mother, everyone expected him to have this incredible determination, like some sense of destiny or something. The truth is he didn't have any idea what his next move would be.

He just wanted to dry off. It's pretty uncomfortable to go around with wet pants and boots.

He drank five beers, and ate some cheese with a little bit of bread. He didn't even try the ham. She barely touched the food.

He was sort of drunk when he said, "Now? This is the way I like the beach: no birds, no people."

9

"What do you think of this?"

With his fists pressed against the ground, he lifted his body up and down, making a perfect right angle with his outstretched legs.

"Come on, try harder, shrimp!" he would say to me.

"I'm trying, asshole!"

I was trying, I really was, but I just couldn't do it like him.

"Don't laugh, man; if you laugh, you won't make it."

Actually, I wasn't laughing at all, but that was all it took. All he had to do was say that, and of course I began to laugh uncontrollably. He knew it. He did it on purpose.

"Come on, cut it out . . ."

"No laughing, now, come on, no laughing. You know what your problem is?"

"No, but I suppose you're going to tell me."

"Well, young man, your problem is that you laugh too much."

He began to laugh, too, but he continued going up and down in the air, as if it were the easiest thing in the world.

"What about you?"

"Me?"

"Yeah, you. You're laughing. Don't hide it."

"Nothing to hide."

He began laughing more and more, and his legs started to shake.

"Hey, Bruce Lee laughs, too," I said.

"No way. Not Bruce Lee."

"Yes he does, he does too."

After that, he couldn't take it anymore, and he fell down onto the floor, howling with laughter. I was laughing, too. We'd been making so much noise that my mother called out from the other room to see what we were doing. Then he got up to take a shower, and I followed him. I got dressed quickly because I wanted him to take me to the mall. I was supposed to meet some guys there to see a movie. Even though he was underage, my mother always let him use the car. Everybody knew he was a hell of a driver, that's why she always let him go. She never let him take it out at night, or go really far away, but the mall was fine.

"I swear this time I'm going to leave without you."

He always said that. But he never once left without me.

"I'm ready!"

We went downstairs to the street. He was wearing his leather boots, and I had mine on, too. We made so much noise with those boots that lots of times the neighbors would come upstairs to complain. But my mother never paid much attention, because she always liked it when we made noise.

A man needs to be heard. It's his nature. Don't ever trust a man who doesn't make any noise.

That's what she always used to say.

I used to call him Bruce Lee, just because I knew he loved it. We both loved Bruce Lee. Actually, we'd only seen one of his movies, on video, but we were hooked all the same. My brother decided after seeing the movie he wanted a body like that, thin but muscular, never beefy, with killer abs. The truth is, little by little, my brother's body was getting there. He had never been like those guys that kill themselves in gym class, though. At all. He'd never even liked sports very much. All he'd wanted was a good body, to be ready, ready for anything.

10

My brother had the gun in the waistband of his jeans, and his black shirt hung down over it, to hide it. His shirtsleeves were rolled way up above his elbows, just like always. He took the gun out and blew the guy's face away. Nobody moved. I know that in the movies, there's always one guy who plays the hero and grabs the gun away from the bad guy and all that shit, but this was real life. In real life when a guy has just blown someone's face off, from less than two feet away, everyone just freezes and shuts up. They were as still and silent as marble statues.

What the fuck? They didn't even know what they'd just seen. Some say there were six guys, others say it was just one. Nobody was brave enough to look him in the face. One woman even said she was sure he was a horrible man.

Horrible?

My brother? I could have died laughing at that one.

"As all of you obviously know, the man I've just killed was no good to anyone. He was not a good person. So let's not get carried away here. I am going to leave here as soon as possible, and if nobody does anything stupid, you can all go on with your afternoons and the rest of your lives in whatever way you see fit."

My brother was quite a public speaker. He always made a good impression.

He went out into the street with the gun in his hand, pointing it at everyone, but not pointing it at anyone, really. He walked toward a car that a family was just getting out of. The father and mother were on the curb already, but there was a girl still in the backseat, putting on lipstick.

"How about giving me those keys," he said to the father, who immediately handed them over, because of the gun, obviously. My brother got in the car, but it wasn't until he looked in the rearview mirror that he noticed her.

"Get out of the car!" he shouted.

"No."

He couldn't spend the whole day arguing, so he started

the car and drove away, fast as hell. The car made a screeching noise as he took off, just like in the movies. That was the first thing he had ever stolen in his whole life. A fucking perfect, brand-new BMW, the pride of German engineering, and with a girl in the backseat.

A very pretty girl.

"Why didn't you get out?" he asked her.

"My father beats me up."

"Maybe I should have killed him, too."

"No, it's better this way. If something happened to my father, I'd think it was my fault, and then I'd be cursed forever. I've begged God a million times to do something, turn him into a quadriplegic, or a vegetable or something. But He's never answered my prayers."

"God doesn't exist."

"Well . . . that explains it, then."

She climbed up to the front seat and sat next to him. For a long time, she just stared at him. You don't usually see guys who drive like that. I don't mean to ignore all that about her father and how he abused her. That was all true, he beat her up pretty bad and even worse afterward, but what I'm saying is that right then and there, she stayed in the car because one look at him and she instantly fell in love with him.

"I knew it would be like that. Not a single cop in sight." He slowed down and drove through the city calmly.

"Don't worry, they'll show up soon enough."

For once in her life, she had a point.

"I have to get out of here. As far away as possible. So I better drop you off somewhere."

"As far away as possible sounds perfect to me. I'll stay with you."

He drove on in silence. He didn't want her to think he was giving in to her, even though he knew he was.

He got lost looking for the highway. He wasn't used to driving in the city. She helped him a little.

I don't think he knew what the hell he was doing. He just wanted to drive and drive and never go back anywhere. He really wasn't a murderer. He was actually sort of a poet. He read a lot.

"Where did you get that gun?"

"I found it."

"Come on . . ."

"I found it in a trash can, I swear. It only has three bullets. Well, two now."

"Did you kill someone?"

"I think so. The security guard at the store, but it was kind of his fault."

"Yeah, I believe it. I've gone into there a million times. God knows how much money I've spent there, and still those security guards make me go through that fucking thing with the receipt every single time. As if I were some kind of thief."

"I know. In my whole life, I've never stolen anything." She smiled.

"Well, not counting this car. But this was an emergency."

She gave him a good, long once-over, and then she smiled again. She was already crazy about him. That wasn't so unusual, though. Girls were always after him. They used to stand by our front door all day long, just waiting for him to come out. He never liked that. In some way, I think it bothered him that he was so good-looking. I don't mean that he wanted to be ugly or anything, but to him, being good-looking was something different, something good, not something you'd use to take advantage. He wasn't one of those guys who used women . . . well, you know what I mean.

He was good-looking. That's all.

"What's it like?"

"What's what like?"

"To kill someone."

"Well, it's sort of like not killing someone, although I suppose it's also a little different."

11

"Careful with that," he said to me. It wasn't the first time I'd ever smoked pot, but this was stronger and I was pretty stoned. He didn't usually smoke when I was around; in fact, that was the first and last time it ever happened.

"I don't like you smoking, you hear? Definitely not this shit. If I see you doing it again, I'll break your arm. Or something worse."

"But it's good stuff."

"I know it's good, just go easy . . . Give it to me now, I don't want you to turn into a moron."

"It's not like it's my first time . . ."

He made like he was going to hit me. Kidding, of course. The truth is, he would never have hit me, no matter what I did.

"Give it to me, shrimp, hand it over now."

I gave it back to him, already dizzy, really gone. My head was already dancing around in some other time zone.

"Do you remember that astronaut they left hanging in space? Was it when Russia collapsed?"

"The Soviet Union, you mean."

"Yeah. Do you remember how nobody wanted to spend the money to get him down and they just left him up there, going around and around in space for a while?"

"Yeah. So?"

"Well, he must have been pretty angry, that guy . . . I don't know why I just remembered him . . . but he must have been pretty pissed off . . . poor Russian."

"Yeah, I bet he won't even climb stairs now."

"No, not even stairs . . ."

"He probably doesn't even have heels on his shoes."

"No way, man . . ."

"I doubt he'll even leave his house again, not even to buy the newspaper."

"No way . . . I bet he just stays at home, chained to the refrigerator."

"They won't ever leave him hanging again."

All of a sudden I started to dance. I don't know why, I just did, right then and there. And I hate dancing. I never do it. Well, that once I did. He just sat there, laughing his head off.

"Keep going, go, go, go . . ."

I'd kept it up, dancing, spinning around and around, waving my arms like crazy. I'm not exactly a professional dancer. He loved it.

"The Dance of the Russian Astronaut! The Russian Astronaut nobody loves!"

He kept egging me on, and I kept on dancing.

"Who loves you, Russian Man?" he called out.

"Nobody, nobody . . ."

"Who's going to get you down from there?"

"Nobody, nobody . . ."

"How do you feel, Russian Man?"

"Alone. All alone."

12

It was our house, and that's what pissed me off. How could they just come into somebody else's house, a house that wasn't theirs, and talk to us like they did?

"All this is fine, ma'am, but while you sit here crying,

your son is out there, beating the shit out of someone. If you don't cooperate, I'm telling you, you're asking for trouble. You, and that little shit"—referring to me, obviously—"and your whole goddamned family."

"I don't know what to tell you. I don't know where he could be. I don't know anything . . ."

"For Christ's sake, this lady's a fucking idiot."

The two cops were in our kitchen. My mother had invited them into the living room, but they didn't even get that far. They started insulting her right then and there. My mother was standing next to the dishwasher, and they just sat themselves down. I was standing in the doorway, half in, half out. I didn't dare leave, but of course I didn't want to go all the way in, either. One of the cops called me over. Not the one who insulted my mother, the other one.

"You, come over here."

I didn't move.

"Now son, you understand that your brother has committed a terrible crime, and that we have to find him before he does something worse."

The other one interrupted him.

"Something worse? Worse than shooting a poor man who didn't do anything to anyone . . . an innocent victim . . . a father . . ."

I found it hard to believe that my brother would shoot someone who hadn't done anything at all.

The policeman kept talking, the calm one, I mean.

"We just want to find him before he hurts himself," he said to me.

The nervous one started to interrupt him again. He really wouldn't let anyone else get a word in.

"Come on! Come on! What kind of a fucking joke is this?"

He jumped out of his chair.

"So he hurts himself, who cares? I don't give a shit if he hurts himself, he can die for all I care—my job is to make sure he doesn't stick that gun in the mouth of another innocent person."

The quieter cop now looked at me as if there was some kind of understanding between the two of us. The truth is, they were doing a pretty good job, but they still didn't fool me. I'd seen that trick before, in the movies. One plays the good cop, the other plays the bad cop. First the bad cop scares you, and then you go tell the whole story to the good cop. This guy was just like the good cop in *Thelma and Louise,* Harvey Keitel's character. Here, the kid was my brother, and, well, you know what happened to poor old Thelma and Louise.

My mother bought the whole act.

"I'll tell you what I know. What else I can do, I don't know, I don't know."

My mother, I mean, she's great-looking and everything, but she just doesn't understand. She didn't get it. Neither of us understood anything, to be honest. My brother had driven off in a car with a girl and a gun. That was all the information available.

When they left the house, the guy playing the "good cop" said to the guy playing the "bad cop":

"This family is a bunch of retards. I have a feeling there's going to be more dead."

At least he was right about that.

My brother once woke up and decided to tape everything he heard people saying on the streets. He had a small Walkman with a microphone that was easy to hide under his clothes. He spent the day walking around, getting on and off buses, walking in and out of all the department stores. Then he went back home. This is what he taped:

"No way . . . maybe . . . It matters to me, too . . . Anything you want . . . Nothing for now, thanks . . . I'm still waiting . . . I don't have the energy . . . I'll give it to you tomorrrow . . . We just don't have the money . . . we just don't have the money . . . we just don't have the money . . . Go away . . . Come here . . . Go away . . . Come back . . . I'm all alone . . . I just don't care anymore . . . We won! . . . The things you say to me! . . . Run, run, run . . . Dogs in my legs and cats in my head . . . It's too late . . . it's too soon . . . You said it . . . All alone, again . . . If he

wasn't so cute . . . God only knows I've tried, I can't tell you how much . . . He doesn't love me . . . two Ds . . . a new job, new shoes, new car . . . I can barely move . . . I'm still young . . . I'm not so young anymore . . . See those two kids, all alone—they must belong to someone . . . I never saw animals like that in the park . . . Is it supposed to rain? . . . They say it's going to rain . . ."

At the beginning and end of the tape, he put:

"I love you . . . I don't love you anymore."

14

For someone who has never noticed things like boots—some have rounded toes and others are pointy, some boots are made of really good leather, and others are fake, and then there are snakeskin boots, and those are the most beautiful things in the world. Just looking at them, they go straight to your head. You get all dizzy, and you feel like you'll never be happy unless you walk through the world in-side of those boots. To someone who's never felt like this, everything I've said and everything I'm about to say—this whole story, in fact—will probably sound like a real freak show.

"Where did you get those boots?"

He lifted up the cuff of his jeans. Just a little, because he wore his black denims tight at the ankle.

"You like them?"

He was just saying that, because he knew that anyone would die for those boots, and he loved it when people said how perfect they were. He never got tired of hearing it. If no one was around, he'd whisper it to himself.

"They're the most beautiful things I've ever seen."

He grinned from ear to ear. He was so fucking proud of those boots.

"Would you ever kill a kid?"

He lowered the cuff of his jeans, and stopped smiling.

"No."

"What about a lady?"

"No. Well . . . I don't know. It depends . . . men and women are the same, when you come down to it . . . I never thought much about killing anyone, to tell the truth."

"But you did . . ."

She talked about killing and dying like other people talk about what to wear to the prom. She didn't know what she was talking about.

"Yeah, I did it . . . but life is kind of strange sometimes. You think it leads you one way, and then all of a sudden it takes you somewhere else, you see it happening, you're in it, but there's nothing you can do to stop it. Like walking on wild horses."

"Would you ever kill an animal?"

"Depends. What kind of animal, what's the situation?"

"How about a horse? A wild horse?"

"That was just a metaphor."

"I *know* it was just a metaphor. What do you think I am, stupid? . . . A dog, then. Would you kill a dog?"

"No."

"What if it was about to eat a little kid? Then would you kill it?"

"I'd fire a warning shot. Scare the dog off. Save the kid."

"You know something? You're an awfully nice person, considering you're a murderer and everything."

She then wiggled into the backseat, to find something in her bag. She took out a pair of sunglasses, put them on, and jumped back into the front seat. She was wearing a pair of cutoffs, and she had these beautiful legs. He caught a glimpse of them for a second, as she did little acrobatics from the back to the front seat of the car. Then he turned his eyes back to the highway.

Like all experienced drivers, he knew that one second of distraction behind the wheel could be lethal. It was just that she had these great legs.

15

The bullet entered his cheek, just above his smile, and then continued up to his brain. On its way out, his cap went with it.

The security guard was on the floor, squirming around. We already know that. Nobody moved. Let's be honest— who really cares about those guards, right? Anyway, he didn't squirm around like that for long. All of a sudden his back arched, like a bow. A bow without an arrow. Useless.

He was dead.

When your brother kills someone, things can get pretty strange. It's not like reading it in the newspaper. The hor- ror oozes into your family and becomes part of it, and that's what changes everything. You don't even know the dead guy. But you do know the killer. I'm not saying I approve, don't get me wrong, I'm just saying that there's two sides to every gun. There's a person at each end, and if the story comes out right, not like they reported it on TV, you'll see how the song changes its tune. Even though, obviously, it's a dead song.

After the guy stopped moving, the people around him stopped playing dead. My brother was already gone by then; it was like he had flown out of there. It all happened so fast. The witnesses started making up these stories about what they thought had happened. Each of them made their own roles bigger than they actually were. It was as if, without *them*, you couldn't truly re-create the scene of the crime. One lady said it was a gang of six men, and that she actually grabbed one, but then he escaped. Another witness said that it was two Chinese guys. Only one witness, a good-looking fortyish lady, got it right, saying that the guy who shot the security guard was very good-looking. This may sound crazy, but that afternoon the police arrested twelve Chinese hoods and five good-looking guys.

None of them looked like him. Not at all.

The truth is, if this hadn't been so horrible, it would've been kind of funny. I'm talking about after the first murder, the way all the witnesses went on television to tell the world about things that didn't even really happen. Making shit up, forgetting what really went on, desperately using that one sad incident to become, for a moment or two, real-life television heroes. Thinking that my brother's gun could change their lives.

It's like all those people in California, waiting for earthquakes.

16

"What do you think?"

She had taken off her blouse to show off her tits, those two tiny, perfect little tits of hers.

"You're very pretty."

"That's it? I'm 'very pretty'? Why didn't you say so before? What do you think of this?" She shimmied to show what she meant. But he didn't even see them—well, maybe a little, but he acted like he was more interested in the highway.

"Can't you slow down a little? Or let's pull over, and we could do something."

"Not yet. When it's safe, I'll stop and we can do whatever you want."

"When it's safe? I'll never be safe with you. You've kidnapped me and you're a murderer and a car thief and God only knows what else!"

"God doesn't exist."

"And an atheist! So you're a murderer, a kidnapper, a thief, an atheist, and probably a rapist, too."

He smiled. She was still topless. It was pretty funny.

"Help, help! Someone save me from the atheist rapist!"

She stuck her head out the window to scream, naked from the waist up, and practically from the waist down, too.

"Help, help! The thief, murderer, rapist, atheist wants to take my body!"

He pretended to get all serious.

"And your soul."

17

I don't think they knew where the fuck they were, but it was a sea of wheat, an endless sea of wheat, and when they climbed onto the roof of the car, him in his black jeans and snakeskin boots, and her in those cutoffs, with that body, she more gorgeous than anything. When they thought, "This is how things should always be," and "This is how things never are," when all they could see was wheat and wheat and nothing more than wheat, while they thought that they loved each other or he thought that he loved her, and maybe even she thought so, too, while the rest of the world thought about something else, something that had to end even before it started, when the world stuck their big fucking noses into that wheat field to see what they were doing, then, right at that moment, they removed themselves, their faces, their bodies, and their love out of the wheat field and they got into the car and started the motor and drove off and didn't look back, not even once.

"Fire" played on the radio.

He said: "Before Hendrix, there was nothing."

Then they fastened their seat belts.

She said: "There's no way to get killed in these European cars."

From far away, you could see the wheat field getting bigger and bigger and at the same time, the two of them getting smaller and smaller.

The clouds, meanwhile, looked like lots of things, and like nothing at all.

18

Nothing, absolutely nothing is dead until it stops moving.

"He stopped moving."

"Looks like it."

He kicked him in the face. Not too hard, though. He was just trying to see if he was really dead.

"He's not going to move."

He stuck the toe of his boot underneath the dead guy's ear. The head bounced a little and then fell back.

"I think he's dead."

She was more scared than a bird in hell. Anybody would've been afraid. What I'm trying to say is that it's not so strange. My brother killed people and it was normal that you'd get scared. She was scared, I was scared, everyone was scared.

"Let's get out of here."

The two of them got back into the car. He started it up and drove without saying anything, until everything was far enough away that it all didn't seem so real.

"You know this song?"

He started singing a John Lennon song, "Woman Is the Nigger of the World."

"No. But it's pretty."

Then they were quiet. They stayed quiet for a while. Everything passed by the car windows, a whole entire world, houses and rivers and factories. There was some kind of connection between all those things, but not with them. You could expect something from every field with tangled trees, but you could also not expect anything at all from the whole package.

"Do you love me?"

She was naked again. She was beautiful, but I've said that before. He didn't know where to look.

"Of course I love you."

"Can I take your word for it? On your honor as a rapist-murderer?"

"Yes."

She showed him the tuft of red hair, curly and perfectly cut, like a lawn of red grass. A small, silent fire.

"See this?"

There was no way not to see it.

"This is all I have, and I'm giving it all to you."

A truck passed by, so close that he swerved to avoid getting hit. The car spun around a few times, and then my brother said:

"It's so pretty that I can't believe it's all yours."

She covered it up like you would guard a treasure.

"Better that way."

According to the TV news reports, they were already dead by then.

19

She was singing something, Sonic Youth, I think. She made these little guitar sounds, like distorted guitars. She sang some of the lyrics and then she did her little guitar thing. She wasn't that bad, actually. When she finished the song, she got all serious, as if she remembered something really sad.

"Know what?"

How could he know? He didn't say anything.

"I was once watching television and I saw this documentary about skinheads. They're the grossest thing in the world, don't you think?"

"I know who they are. I wish I never heard of them."

"Well, me neither, but the thing is, the documentary was all about this group of them living in Alabama. They were all real little kids, some of them weren't even ten years old, and then there were some a few years older, and they all had these tattoos of swastikas and wore combat boots and suspenders and Hitler T-shirts, and all that stuff. They lived with this guy named Riccio or something. He was old and he took care of them all. He showed them videos, like lots of World War II stuff, and all the kids ended up about as crazy as he was. They were like one big family of psychos."

"Like a big pile of shit is more like it."

"Um . . . that too. But the thing that got me was that the kids there had all run away from home, their parents beat them up and stuff. Everyone said that the old Nazi guy was very good to them, and they all loved each other very much even though they hated Jews and blacks and everything. It was like, first nobody loved them, and then there they were, waiting in line for their rifles."

"It's always the same old story. I've heard it before. Don't take it too literally. I mean, there's always been mother-fuckers like that."

"I'm not saying I *believe* any of it, I'm just pointing out that it's always the abused dogs who bite back."

"Yeah, but they never bite their masters back."

He then rounded a curve, accelerating so fast it was like he wanted to scare himself. When the road straightened out, he went even faster, as fast as the car would go. I don't think he would've cared if he killed himself right then and there. He was sick of it. Sick of listening to all that talk. Sick of all the stories. Sick of how predictable things were. Sick of how things couldn't be any other way.

He stuck his head out the window and felt the wind on his face. He was going so fast he could barely breathe.

we're all in this **together**

20

"The truth is, it's all the same to me if he goes around killing people. I also killed a guy once, but I'm allowed to. That's the law. I can, but he can't. Things are funny that way. I don't want to have to catch him, but I don't have a choice. Know what I mean?"

After the good cop/bad cop, they sent over the smart cop/stupid cop team. That was the smart one.

"What the fuck are you saying?"

That was the stupid one.

"Are all these books his?"

The smart one was okay; he reminded me a little of Harry Dean Stanton.

"Yeah. He reads a lot, and writes, too. Poetry."

"Right. This guy's no idiot. It's going to make it that much harder."

He scanned the bookshelf, with interest; the other cops had gone right past it, as if it were a brick wall. They were just looking for drugs, or weapons, or magazines with naked guys. They were all convinced he was a fag, just because. I think it was because they all hated how good-looking he was. And also so they could go home feeling that their daughters were all safe.

"Hey, kid. You sure you don't know where he is?"

The stupid one.

"No, Officer, I don't. I already told you everything, I've told everybody everything I know, a thousand times."

That was true. I was starting to get tired of all the police, and all these interviews. Having a murderer for a brother can get kind of tiring after a while.

"Let me tell you something. I'd rather be reading poetry than chasing after people like I do. In this type of work, nobody ever wants to see you. My wife told me that. You know she left me because I smelled like a cop? That's what she told me. You smell like a cop. Can you believe it? I don't even know what a cop smells like. Come over here—do you smell anything? Garbage? Fish? What the hell do I smell like? Here, come over—what do you think?"

He stuck his jacket sleeve in front of me, and moved a little closer. I sniffed him a little. It felt sort of silly.

"What is it?"

"Nothing. It doesn't smell like anything."

That was true. It smelled sort of like cigarettes, but that was about it.

"I don't know . . . she must have had some kind of supersensitive nose. Smelled like a cop! No goddamned joke."

Meanwhile, the stupid cop started smelling himself. After a few sniffs, he seemed satisfied.

"You know, I once tried to kill my wife. No kidding. I took out my gun and I stuck it right to her head. You know what it feels like to have a gun on you?"

"No."

"You want to try it?"

Well, now that he suggested it, I *was* kind of curious, so I moved a little closer to him. He took out his silver automatic, and pressed it against my temple. It was cold.

"I swear I wanted to kill her. I wanted her dead, rubbed out, like you rub out a stain or a spelling mistake. That's what my wife was to me—a mistake, one big unbearable mistake."

The stupid cop, I noticed, was starting to get nervous. Not me. I was totally cool. I knew he had no intention of killing me, and anyway, the more I looked at him, the more he looked like Harry Dean Stanton.

"All right, all right, that's good enough. Let's get on with this."

He put his automatic back in his holster.

"So did you kill her?"

"No, son, I didn't. I never seem to do the things I really want to do, but that's life, I guess. And I don't want to have to kill your brother, because I'm sure he's a nice kid, and he reads poetry and anyway I know those security guards are a pain in the ass, but it's not like I have a choice. I know I'm going to have to go out there and bring him in. Maybe I'll have to kill him. Who knows? I mean, you can see how fucked-up this is. First, I want to kill my wife and now I might have to kill your brother."

It didn't bother me that he said that. It really didn't. It may sound strange, but I think he was just being honest. And he really did look just like Harry Dean Stanton.

21

After he shot the guard, there was a dark moment, completely black. It was as if he had shot himself in the face. He couldn't feel his own hand, and he couldn't feel the weight of the gun either. Then his sight came back. The first thing he saw was all the scared people in front of him, except they didn't look like people, they didn't have anything to do with what he'd seen before. Everything else—the cash register, the cans of food, the magazines on the racks—everywhere he looked, things seemed newborn, brand-new. Even ordinary things looked like new inventions, things he'd never seen before. Every step he then took toward the exit seemed like a baby step, and every breath he took felt like brand-new fresh air. When he finally saw himself in the mirror that ran alongside the glass door, he was struck by how different yet so vaguely familiar he seemed. He almost said hello to the person staring back at him.

He also couldn't help feeling a little bit satisfied knowing that he was the one still alive; it was the other guy who was dead.

22

"And if it touches one of us, it touches all of us. And if one of us is happy, all of us are happy, and we laugh together and we cry together. Why?"

"BECAUSE WE'RE ALL IN THIS TOGETHER!"

Welcome to the exciting, wonderful world of the family. The host of *We're All in This Together* spoke to us and the audience, but mainly, she looked straight into the camera. She was one of those ladies who would've been really ugly if she weren't so rich. Her clothes and stage makeup transformed her, so that at first, she was actually kind of attractive. But if you looked at her a little closer, then you'd see how ugly she really was. Close up, her appeal melted away, like an ice cream in a microwave.

It was hot as hell in there.

"If one person dies, all of us die; if one person suffers, all of us suffer . . . and if one of us kills"—she said this for our benefit—"we are all killers. And why is that, ladies and gentlemen?"

The studio audience all answered in unison.

"BECAUSE WE'RE ALL IN THIS TOGETHER!"

The premise of this particular talk show was to promote family unity. Every week they featured guests, families that had either suffered some devastating trauma, or had something good happen to them. Either good or bad, the purpose was to demonstrate how one person's experience always had an impact on the entire family. The show's opening sequence had these little animated dominoes that fell, one by one, after the first one was knocked down.

My mother looked stunning, as usual. We went on a lot of talk shows, I think, just because we were such a good-looking family. They insisted on making me up so I would look like a real juvenile delinquent. The makeup lady messed up my hair and the wardrobe people made me take off my brother's leather jacket and put on a brand-new red one, which was pretty cool, but definitely too new. Like, it wasn't broken in or anything. The talk-show host said it was my brother's jacket on the air. That pissed me off, but I didn't say a word. In fact, I didn't open my mouth during the entire show. My mother, on the other hand, was busy trying to convince the audience that in spite of everything, she was a good mother, and I was a good kid, and the whole thing with my brother was just an isolated incident. Nobody bought it, though.

BECAUSE WE'RE ALL IN THIS TOGETHER.

Before the show began, the camera crew set up and the director explained to the audience what they were supposed to do. While we were waiting backstage, I made friends with this girl, she was about ten. Her father had taken off all his clothes, climbed up to the roof of their house with a shotgun, and then opened fire on the people down in the street. He didn't hurt anyone, but they locked him up in a mental hospital somewhere. The girl, her brother, and her mother were standing around in the hallway.

My mother and I were the main attraction of the program, so we had a little dressing room to ourselves, with a minibar and a fruit-and-cheese platter.

I asked the little girl if she wanted to check out our dressing room, and when she saw what they'd given us, she seemed kind of shocked.

"Why'd they give you all that? We didn't get anything."

The little girl was obviously disappointed.

"I don't know. I guess because my brother had better aim than your father."

23

"Dying isn't such a big deal."

The sun flattened everything, like an elephant's foot.

"Dying is like being inside the train when it's already passed your stop."

"What the hell are you talking about?"

She didn't like it when he talked that way. Neither did I.

"It's just something I read. A poem by Robert Lowell."

"You read poetry?"

"Sometimes."

"Do you write poetry, too?"

"No. Never."

"Would you write a poem for me?"

"No. If you want a poem, you better write it yourself. I've already got enough on my mind."

He lifted his shirt and for a split second, the gun was exposed. Then he lowered his shirt and the gun was hidden again. Someone waved at him from the highway. One hundred birds started flying around a lamppost, and then one hundred bats, and then it was night and you couldn't see a thing.

"I can't see a thing."

He put on his brights. A little further up, they realized that there still wasn't much of anything. They drove past a police car. They were going fast, but the police didn't move.

"They'll never catch us."

She didn't know what she was talking about, and he knew she didn't know what she was talking about.

"You don't know what you're talking about."

She kissed him, and for a second he couldn't see the highway. He felt her tongue in his mouth, and then he felt something strange on the tip of his dick, like when you touch a dog's nose.

When they finally pulled over, it was so late, and so dark, that they could have been anyone, in any car. Everything they said and everything they did disappeared, as if they were nothing, and they were saying nothing. Then she said: "I love you."

They fell asleep after that, right away.

24

He parked the car away from the bar, because he was afraid someone might notice it. Before he had even turned off the motor, she jumped out of the car, like a little girl. Like a happy little girl, not scared or anything.

He ordered a beer and she ordered an ice cream and a Coke. It was hot, and the bar was just about empty. There was just an older guy, a traveling salesman, eating at one of the tables. He looked like one of those salesmen you always see in the movies.

He finished his beer and ordered another. He loved beer. He could drink about a hundred of them without ever getting drunk. She was still licking her ice-cream cone, studying the tapes and CDs in the display counter, the kind they always have at those places off the highway. He was looking at her. The waiter was looking at her, too.

"Going somewhere?"

He didn't feel much like talking. My brother wasn't the

kind of guy who talked to people on elevators, but it would be kind of strange not to answer the waiter.

"Yeah, we're going somewhere."

"Where to?"

She answered this time.

"Czechoslovakia!"

"Fuck, that's a long ways from here."

He laughed. She moved over to him, and kissed him on the cheek.

"We're going to get married in Prague."

"Yeah. We're going to Prague to get married."

Usually, he didn't like playing make-believe like that, but with her it seemed fun.

"You two seem pretty young to be getting married."

"Well, we're not going to get married right away, you see. First, we'll get to Prague, then we'll get settled in. We'll wait until we're mature enough to take the next step, to solidify the relationship, you know? Once we've taken that step, we'll be ready to unite our lives, you know, into one common destiny."

I guess that at that point, the waiter realized they were bullshitting him, but he was too bored and too stupid to stop.

"That sounds good . . . but why Prague, why don't you wait right here and do it?"

"Because Prague is where Kafka waits."

The waiter then turned away, busying himself with lots of little things all at once, as if the diner got really busy all of a sudden. It was as if he'd never spoken with them at all.

She paid for the beers, the Coke, and the ice cream, and then he bought a couple more beers.

"I've got money, don't worry about it. Let me pay for it. Yesterday was my birthday, and instead of a present my father gave me money. A lot. He says that he gives me money because he never knows what I want."

"I guess you just want him to stop beating you up."

"No, no . . . I don't want to bring up that stuff. I just hope that maybe one day people will say about me, 'She could tell some pretty sad stories, but she never did.' I think that's about the best thing you can say about someone."

He went over near the counter with the CDs and tapes, and came back with a pink hat with a paper flower on the brim. It was a pretty dumb-looking hat, but then, what the hell would he know about hats. On her, it looked beautiful.

"Happy birthday."

She kissed him again, this time on the lips.

He paid for the hat and they went outside. He left a big tip on their way out. Afterward, on the evening news, the waiter swore they stole four beers, a Coke, and a pink hat.

Nobody was able to locate the salesman.

25

She was completely naked, but he still had his jeans on.

"Don't you want to touch me?"

They parked the car near a river. The water trickled by, making only a faint sound.

"I guess so."

He was a virgin—well, that's what I think, and that's what I've said before, even though there's no way to be completely sure of something like that. I think he was a virgin, I know he was a virgin although I don't know how or why I know. Maybe it's because I am, too.

She started by unzipping his jeans. I think he must've been pretty uncomfortable without his jeans, because before taking them off she'd have to take off his boots. And I know he hated taking off his boots.

"Do you like this?"

She was touching him. She told me. She had such a nice body. So did he, the two of them were so good-looking.

Then he kissed her and they went on like that for a

while, touching, and then I guess they did it. She told me they did it, and she told me *how* they did it, too.

He couldn't do anything at first, I mean, he couldn't get it up. Then it was okay, after she had put him in her mouth.

He seemed to know he didn't have much time left. He touched her all over, like you touch something you know you're going to miss. She came first. He came too, but it took a little while. It was only after she whispered: "Come on, give it to me, give it to your little whore."

Then he kissed her, all over her forehead, and all over her body, and he stroked her hair, and the back of her neck, until they both fell asleep. Him first and then her.

When they woke up, she told him about the dream she had had. They had a tiny little house in the middle of a field full of trees and flowers and the sky wasn't the color of sky, it was more white. It was as if it were going to snow even though it was hot out, not boiling hot, just a breezy heat that you feel on your arms when you leave an air-conditioned movie theater in the middle of the summer.

He said he couldn't remember his dream at all, except that it was cold, much colder than an air-conditioned movie theater and even colder than snow.

As he put on his black jeans and his boots, she thought about all the men who'd ever touched her before, and then she thought about all the men who would touch her after him and put their things inside of her. She decided he would always be the most important. The one the others would be afraid of.

26

"You know I once broke a man's arm after cuffing him?"

It was the smart cop talking. He came by again to pay a short visit. My mother was out. She was on a radio show; the topic was women who'd been abandoned by their husbands. After hearing her story, I bet men would think twice before dumping their wives. The stupid cop didn't come over so it was just the two of us, me and the smart cop. We sat down in the living room, and I brought him a beer. I had one, too. I didn't bother with glasses. We drank from the cans.

"It was pretty easy—I put my foot against the guy's back, and pulled his arm until I heard it crack. The sound was what got to me, I've never broken anything before. He was howling, like some kind of animal. He was one of those guys that goes around parks, molesting little kids. I figured he deserved a broken arm. At least."

"Yeah, sounds fair to me."

"See? That's something that most people don't understand. We can't let people like that just walk the streets, molesting small children. Children are sacred."

"Yeah. I agree."

"That's exactly it, and that's why I'm not interested in chasing your brother down. He's not hurting little kids."

I know my brother; he'd never touch a little kid.

"He'd never touch a little kid."

"I know that, and I don't want to have to go out there and blow his head off, but, you know, your brother . . . he's a little unstable. Kind of disturbed, but disturbed in a different way, and that's the problem here. It's not good."

He sat there, silent for a while. Looking at the floor. Then he lifted his head.

"No . . . not good at all."

He looked terrible. I think all this must have really gotten to him. He was a nice guy, and I understood him when he talked to me.

I went to the kitchen for two more beers. My mother hated it when we drank in the house, but I guess at this point, what difference did it make?

I gave him his beer. He opened it, and then I opened mine.

"Thanks. Your family . . . you're all such nice people, so nice-looking, too. Your mother's very pretty, if you don't mind my saying so."

"No, no, go ahead."

I was putting on a little bit of an act, like, nothing-surprises-me-anymore. Although, it was kind of true. My brother killed people, and nothing surprised me anymore.

"So nice-looking . . . you too, all of you are so nice-looking. And him, he's the best-looking one of the bunch, that's for sure. Killing him's the last thing I want to do."

He was silent again. He held his face in his hands, and he looked like he was about to cry.

He suddenly snapped out of it.

"Is there any more beer left?"

I finished the one I had in one gulp. Then I went into the kitchen and took two more cans out of the refrigerator.

I returned with the beer, and we drank in silence. He didn't say anything else. When he was about to leave, he looked at me as if we were really good friends. I felt good. Even though I was a little drunk, and I felt okay right then. I liked the idea of having a friend who could break some- one's arm if they tried to hurt me.

"Listen, kid, I swear to God I'm not liking this at all, but it's out of my hands. I'm probably going to have to kill your brother."

He rested his hand on my shoulder, as if we were old high school buddies, or even better, two old cops.

"I understand. Don't worry about it."

I think he was telling the truth.

27

"If someone tried to come at me with a knife, what would you do?"

"I'd kill him with my gun."

"If someone tried to rape me and then made me swear not to say anything, what would you do?"

"I'd kill him with my gun."

"If someone hurt me, really hurt me so that, in like a thousand years I'd still never forget it, what would you do?"

"I'd kill him with my gun."

Along both sides of the road, the trees and telephone wires ran parallel with the cars. There was nothing close to them anymore, nothing new, nothing old, nothing ahead, and of course, nothing, absolutely nothing behind.

Just this.

28

They were in the middle of a forest. The trees arched over the long thin road. It had stopped raining, and everything was still wet. Soon it would be nighttime; it was that time of day when everything seems both real and strange at the same time.

They got out of the car and started to walk. She was a little cold so he took off his black shirt for her to wear. He still had a black T-shirt on. She felt the tall, wet grass brush against her legs as she walked. He didn't feel the grass at all; he only heard it as it brushed against his boots.

"If you could only do one more thing in your life, what would it be?"

"Nothing."

"Nothing?"

"Yeah. Nothing."

"What's so good about doing nothing?"

"Well, there's nothing bad about it."

I don't think she really understood him. She just looked

at his body, underneath his black T-shirt, and thought about how sexy he was. She wasn't able to understand that all he really wanted was to be left alone. Alone and away from any confrontations or obligations, from everything good and from everything bad, too.

"Nothing. Yes sir. That's all I want out of life. Nothing."

"Nothing at all?"

"Nothing nothing nothing nothing nothing nothing nothing nothing."

He was impossible sometimes.

She found a little path then, and they started to climb, first up a stone walkway and then up a wooden stairway. It was all wet and warped and crooked. It was so crooked that you couldn't imagine being satisfied after building such a rickety stairway; so crooked only an idiot could have built it; so crooked that she thought to herself, "Whoever lives on the other side of this stairway must be out of his mind."

At the end of the stairway, there was a house, in the middle of the forest. It was as broken-down as the stairway. A small wooden house that looked like you could knock it over with a sneeze. There were brightly colored curtains, and a big, frightened dog sat in the window. The whole place looked ready to fall apart.

A handwritten For Sale sign was posted up on a tree. The lettering was faded from the rain. A couple finally emerged, at the top of the stairs.

"Hello there. Would you like to see the house?"

The man stood in front, wearing a worn-out blue polo shirt and a pair of torn jeans. He looked pretty strong. Behind him was a woman, who had short brown hair and a black eye.

"Come up. Won't you please join us?"

They both thought it was funny how he spoke so formally, even though he looked like a dumb brute who couldn't even put two pieces of wood together to build a decent stairway.

"All of this is ours . . . and it could be yours."

The house was surrounded by a fence, and the green and vacant forest was just beyond it.

"Did you build it yourself?"

"Yes sir. With my own two hands."

He held up his hands and everyone, including his wife, looked at them for a while. She was small, and she looked scared, about as scared as the dog, which was big.

"Come in, please come in."

They went inside, and the floorboards creaked like the floors of a boat. The windows were small like the windows on a boat, and it was dark inside.

"It feels like a boat."

"It may feel like a boat, ma'am, but it's not."

She thought it was strange that this woman called her ma'am, since she was only seventeen. The man was old; he was around twenty-seven or twenty-eight.

The woman looked around fifteen but she could've just as well been thirty.

"We've been very happy here."

As you walked in there was a tiny room with a kitchen table and a TV set, with a VCR resting on top of it. There were videos piled up: cartoons, some sports. Then they went into a dark bedroom; on the bed there was a bedspread with zebra stripes.

She whispered to him:

"This is like a kids' tree house or something."

Right then, a little boy jumped out of a closet. A small blond boy that looked like the man, but seemed as frightened as the woman and the dog.

"Why don't we have a drink in the living room?"

They went back into the tiny living room and sat around the table. The television was on. The reception was terrible; the images that jumped around the screen were so fuzzy that you couldn't see anything.

"It's broken. It's the only thing in here that doesn't work; everything else works like clockwork."

The scared, short woman with brown hair smiled, and the strong man placed three glasses on the table, then filled them with wine. They each had a glass, except for her.

"So . . . would you like to buy the house?"

They didn't know what to say. It was all so eerie, like everything. They drank the wine and then the man poured more, and they drank that too, and more after that, until they finished the bottle.

"I think we have to go now."

"So . . . how do you like it?"

My brother was confused.

"It's great . . . umm . . . we do like it. Maybe we'll come back later to make an offer."

"Don't you want to know the asking price?"

The house was so small that they were already outside when he mentioned the price.

"Oh, no. I'm sure we'd never be able to pay what it's really worth."

They turned and went down the soft, crooked wooden

steps and then the crooked stone steps, and when they got to the bottom, she said to him:

"You should have killed him."

He knew he should have killed the man. He was so ashamed that he couldn't say a thing. He got in the car, started the engine, and took off. He didn't want to know anything else about the little house in the forest, the bad man, his scared wife, and the boy in the closet.

29

"God isn't on our side."

He knew his luck was running out.

"There's no way you can know something like that," she said to him.

Boy, she really didn't understand anything.

"Don't you see, God can't side with killers, he's never sided with killers; he believes in that cheek thing."

"That's Jesus," she said. "God had already killed a ton of people by the time Christ came. What about the plagues, or Babel, or the floods. We could never kill as many people as He killed with the floods."

She didn't know the Old Testament very well. In fact, she'd only flipped through one of those children's Bibles once or twice, when she was a little girl. Now she reads everything: the Bible, the Koran, a little about Buddhism, and a lot about black magic. She told me that herself. She still writes to me, wherever she is, and tells me about her life now; she also tells me stories about my brother and the trip she took with him, after the shooting. She tells me about what they did and what they talked about, and how she felt throughout the whole thing. She's far away now, but that's another story altogether.

"In the beginning, God was a beast."

"Yeah. I guess they changed their politics after a while. I mean, He couldn't have been too popular, after the plagues and the floods and everything."

She tried to imagine what God looked like and for a moment, she thought He should be an old woman, with sweet slanted eyes instead of an Aryan white motherfucker with a beard down to the ground.

30

Her kisses woke him up. She was kissing him, first his tight stomach, then his chest, and finally his lips. He was asleep, with his pants and his boots on. It was pretty hot when he woke up. He couldn't even imagine what time it was, eleven or twelve, or maybe even earlier. She was sleeping beside him, in a Michael Jackson T-shirt with nothing underneath.

My brother and I always liked Michael Jackson, a lot. We never believed that rumor about him and the little boy. Not for a second.

My brother sat there, staring at that T-shirt, still half asleep. Almost as if instead of sleeping with her, he had been sleeping with Michael.

"So you got married," he said. He was talking about how Michael had married Elvis's daughter.

"Yes sir, I've married the King's daughter."

"Well, now you have it all: the Beatles' music and Elvis

Presley's daughter. I guess there's nobody in the world who can top you now."

She started kissing him again. He realized that he had been talking to her, and that he'd been sleeping with her, and that she was just about all he had in the world.

31

He drove the car past a massive factory, a cement or lime-stone or some factory like that. It was a huge building covered with pipes, coated in a white powder. There was a big group of workers there, all covered in the same white powder, taking a lunch break or changing shifts or something. The car went by so fast that my brother couldn't do anything to help them and they didn't have a chance to help him, either.

And then he was gone.

32

It was getting darker. There were no clouds in the sky. No houses. There was nothing.

"Where are we going to sleep?"

He turned his head and looked at her, shocked. He could have sworn he was all alone in the car.

33

My mother and I were home alone. The television was on, but the volume was so low that we couldn't really hear anything. There were some dogs on the screen, doing some tricks. First, really stupid house tricks like fetching the newspaper or a pair of slippers and all that stuff, but then, all of a sudden they flashed their teeth and started attacking this dog trainer who was wearing one of those rubber suits. My mother was flipping through her appointment book. We were getting a lot of invitations to all sorts of TV programs and radio shows, as well as newspaper and magazine interviews. One of them actually offered my mother money to pose naked. She said no, of course. She didn't even mention that one to me; I only found out when they called back to up their initial offer. My mother was busy keeping track of all the dates and appointments, deciding which programs she wanted to appear on, and which ones she didn't.

I begged her to tell them I was sick or something. It wasn't true of course, but I just wasn't having fun with it anymore; the TV, the radio, and all the newspapers, I was tired of them. I had talked so much about my brother that he was turning into some sort of stranger. I started to think, if I ever got to see him again, I'd probably feel like the brother of a rock star. I'd be like something he left behind, someone he'd barely even remember. It would be sort of like being Madonna's brother.

My mother kept herself busy, clipping all the newspaper and magazine articles, and taping all of our TV appearances. By then, I think she had gone a little crazy.

The telephone rang, over the weak barks of the dogs on television. My mother didn't move, so I got up to answer it.

"I'm sorry kid, I had to do it."

I hung up. My mother finished jotting something down in her date book and looked up. She was waiting to hear who called.

"It was my friend. The cop. He says he killed my brother."

The dogs on the TV were quieter now, but they were still looking at the guy in the rubber suit with a vague sense of suspicion.

god's greatest **hits**

34

The sky was filled with white lights, small ones, like tiny flares. Then some silvery rockets appeared out of nowhere, moving in a zigzag. Next, a pair of red and yellow rockets sailed straight up, and burst into an illuminated, starry umbrella. After each explosion, tiny little flames trickled down, disappearing just before they reached the ground. There was a pause, just before the grand finale. Suddenly, everything they had been watching, one by one, rained down, and for a split second it felt like war, you know, the kind you see on TV. Like when the Americans bombed Iraq and all you could see were endless colors, no dead people, nothing. The noise then stopped, and the flames disappeared. People kept staring at the sky. But there was nothing left.

"What did you think of that?" he asked her.

She had her sunglasses on, as if she had been watching them test the atomic bomb.

"Cool. Usually I think fireworks are boring, but these were really good."

"At least it was short. I hate it when they drag it out, making you wait, and then it's one after the other after the other and it's hours before you see anything good."

"I know what you mean. If you're going to do it, do it fast."

"Exactly. Do you want a drink?"

"Yeah, let's get a drink. Then we can go dancing."

"I don't dance."

That was true, we never danced.

"Well, I'll find someone else, then."

She said that sort of thing to make him jealous, but he didn't even notice. He didn't think of her as his girlfriend, or anything. All the people who had been watching the fireworks were wandering around the fair. The food booths were full, and so were all the little rides, like the miniature waterwheels and miniature merry-go-rounds.

They squeezed through the crowd and up to one of the counters at the bar. He ordered two beers, and then before paying, ordered two more.

"We better get a bunch now. We'll never make it back here again."

The crowds were so tightly packed that it was almost impossible to walk without stepping on someone or getting bumped by someone walking by. Yet, he felt strangely calm in the middle of all these people. The more people there were, the less chance anyone would notice him.

"Look! Air guns! Let's shoot!"

"I don't like those rifles. They're fake."

I guess he'd feel sort of dumb playing with a fake gun after he'd fired a real one and killed a man the day before. They sat down in the grass, near one of those machines with a mechanical witch that tells fortunes. A few little boys stood there, staring at the witch, and when she started to move, they screamed in laughter and fright, at the same time.

He knew that he had the gun, tucked into his waistband; so did she. It made them both feel protected. It was like when we were kids and we slept with a pair of wooden broomsticks under the bed.

When they finished the first two beers they started on the next two. She lay down in the grass and rested her head between my brother's legs. He'd never had a girlfriend before, so this seemed like a good thing. She tells me that he caressed her hair, but I'm not so sure about that. In all the years I lived with him, I never saw him caress anyone's hair. Not even once.

As they fell asleep, they heard the little boys and the witch. They were both exhausted. After a little while, the fair was over, and when they woke up, nobody was there at all.

The sun was coming up, so they got up, got into the car, and left. She crawled onto the backseat and went on sleeping while he drove toward the sea.

She loved the sea, she dreamt about it, about the beach and the sand. In her dream, she was alone with her mother and a bunch of little boys who were her brothers. She tells me she always wanted a lot of brothers. She dreamt that she was buried in the hot sand, just like when she was a little girl. When the waves reached her, buried under the sand, at first she was scared that she was going to drown. But then, all of a sudden she found that she could breathe under water. Just like that.

. . .

A gunshot woke her up.

As she stuck her head out the window, she saw they were at a gas station. When she looked down at the ground, she saw a man shrieking and wiggling around like a lizard, his face covered with blood. My brother was standing over him, with the gun in his hand. No one else was there.

He realized that he had woken her up.

"Sorry."

He went over to the pump and took the gas cap off. As he filled the tank, the man's shrieks grew weaker and weaker, until finally they stopped.

"He's not moving."

"He won't."

He started the car.

"He said something about calling the police. I guess they've been talking about me on TV."

"About us, you mean."

She didn't know what to think. That's what she tells me, that she never, ever saw anyone bleeding and screaming like that. She had also never seen a dead guy before.

"Are you going to keep on killing people like this?"

"No. I don't think so. I've only got one bullet left."

It started getting hot. Humid hot. They were getting close to the sea now. He loved the sea. I already mentioned that. What he didn't like was the beach.

35

Twenty miles after the second murder, there was a clap of thunder. Twenty miles; she was counting. After a while, she heard it again. It was closer this time. The sky finally turned black and it started to rain. It was eight-thirty in the morning, but it felt more like the middle of the night.

She was scared.

"Aren't you scared?"

"Of what? The thunder?"

"Of everything."

"I don't know, I don't feel anything. Have you ever been to a funeral?"

"About a year ago. For my grandfather."

"Do you remember how it feels, right when they lower the coffin in the ground? It's like a void, not sad, or happy, or anything. You know what I mean?"

"Yeah, I do."

"Well, that's how I feel. I don't know if it's fear or what, but right now, that's all I can feel."

It was getting darker and darker, and it was raining harder and harder. The thunder was getting closer. I think he realized that he couldn't go on with her in that storm. He couldn't let her go where he was going. He couldn't let her end up like he was going to end up.

36

"When I was a little girl, I was always climbing, way up high. Telephone poles, cranes, balconies, stuff like that. I always wore black gloves. I'd climb to the top with my gloves, and I'd look down over everything. I slept with my gloves, ate with my gloves. I wouldn't take them off for anything. My mother wouldn't hold my hand when we went places. She hated my gloves. But I was crazy about them."

"Leather gloves?"

"Yeah. Black leather gloves. Lined with chamois."

"I had ones like that, too."

"You're kidding. Really? With *yellow* chamois?"

"Yellow chamois."

"Weird. You really must be sent straight from heaven,

just for me. I mean, not too many little kids wear black leather gloves."

My brother used to wear leather gloves all the time until he was thirteen. Then one day he stopped wearing them.

"What happened to your gloves?"

He had thrown them out of a train window. I don't remember where we had been going, but I do remember seeing his gloves flying through the air, like two amputated hands.

"I lost them," he said.

"Come on, nobody loses gloves like that. What did you really do with them? I burned mine. Well, my mother insisted I throw them out. She wanted to take me to a psychiatrist because of the whole thing, so instead I just burned them. My mother said she hated my gloves, and I said to her: "'My gloves are my hands.'"

37

"Hit me."

They were both naked. He was still inside of her. He stopped moving. I guess he must've been scared.

He was scared. She told me so.

"Come on, hit me."

He pulled out of her, but she grabbed him and squeezed it hard, with both hands. He didn't say anything. I don't know if he liked it or what.

"Hit me."

They were leaning against the car. It was almost night-time. You could see the cars on the highway and just over their heads planes swooped down, on their way into the air-port. It was hot, and both of them were sweating. He could hear James Brown on the radio, and he also heard her, up close. He looked at his dick, sitting in her hand, as if it were someone else's dick, or nobody's dick at all. A trapped dick.

"Hit me."

On the other side of the highway, there was a wheat field. A little further up, a green gas station. The sky was blue on top, and yellow on the bottom. Her skin was white, and her cheeks sort of red. It was as if she'd just run through a field of wheat in the hot sun, out of breath.

He looked away from the planes and the cars and the gas station and stood there staring at her face, her eyes, her lips, that peculiar way she moved her mouth. It was a strange face, not like any face he had ever seen before.

"Hit me."

He lifted his hand and she closed her eyes, anticipating the blow.

38

The sun came in through the open windows, just like the wind, and it blew her hair backward and forward, and it wasn't hot and it wasn't cold and it wasn't early and it wasn't late and they drank beer and the road had no end and it really sounded like God was finally playing all his greatest hits.

39

"When I was little I believed in God."

"So what happened?"

"Nothing, that was the problem. It didn't seem like God really took care of me all that much, so I just kind of stopped thinking about Him. Now, it's like, I don't believe in Him but I don't *not* believe in Him, either. Because *I'm* the one who really takes care of me."

"That's the way it should be."

"I don't know . . . sometimes I think God exists for everyone else, and that for some reason, He can't be bothered with me. Or that maybe there *is* a God, but He just isn't as, you know, capable as they say He is. Or maybe God's a little slow, or a little bit lost, or a little stupid."

"God? Stupid?"

"Yeah, why not? Like the president, you know? I've thought about this before—maybe there's this smarter, alternate God, waiting in the wings somewhere, but since our God is immortal and everything, the smart one will never get His chance. I mean, maybe the whole world is like . . . Mexico. In Mexico, it's always the same story . . . no matter what happens, it's always the same rich scumbags running everything."

"We could join the Zapatistas."

"Yeah, and we could also go to the moon and walk all over Neil Armstrong's footprints."

"I have a feeling that you and me and Mexico are going to have to wait a long, long time before the stupid God resigns."

40

"Do you ever tell lies?"

"No . . . not really . . . not at all in fact."

"Really? I'm always lying to people, to everyone, anyone. If I ever told the truth, my life would be frightening. I'd be dead. A beautiful, wonderful, honest, dead girl."

"What kind of lies?"

"What kind? Every kind there is. They come in all

shapes and all sizes: little white lies, big whoppers, subtle lies, obvious lies, lies that I have a good reason for, lies that are pointless, lies that hurt, and lies that heal."

"Lies that heal?"

"Yeah. Lies that can heal the soul."

He slowed down as they approached a small town, and then he accelerated again. They passed a series of high-tension towers, the kind that look like skinny giants made of wire. The fields were filled with these towers, hundreds of them leading up to a central power station.

"I want to be a model, and a singer, and an astronaut . . . no, fuck that. I mean, I already know I'm pretty . . . I want to write music, that's it, I want to be a songwriter, or maybe not . . . maybe there's already enough songs out there. I want everyone to look at me, and love me, and I want them to rape me, I want them to stalk me and kill me in the street . . . I once wrote a song about a guy who couldn't hold anything with his hands. Everything was within his reach, but he just couldn't get anything. His hands were like ripped fishnets. I once told everyone that my mother was a movie star, and that I had twelve brothers and that on my birthday my father bought me a horse and that I had a boyfriend, a boyfriend that I don't have, and that he really loved me, and that he had a really big dick, so big that it choked me, and he had an airplane, and a star, and his own road that only he knew about and green eyes and black hair, hair as black as your gun."

"So what happened?"

He was speeding. He was escaping, really, so it was logical that he'd be speeding. He kept going faster and faster, and he liked it like that. Both of them did.

"Well, it's all right here. I never go anywhere without my lies."

She tried looking out the window, but everything was going by so fast that it wasn't even worth looking. She stared at him. He was calm, sitting there behind the wheel. He didn't have anywhere to go, and there was nowhere he even wanted to go. She didn't really care that much, either.

"I love my lies, you know. They're all I have."

Right then, they sped past a boy on a bike, a thin boy wearing a red cap. She thought of something, and had the feeling that he was thinking about the same thing. They then both forgot what they were thinking about and they left the boy on the bike behind and he slowly disappeared, like so many other things that could have changed everything forever.

41

"I just realized that I stopped thinking about what the rest of my life will be like. I don't know exactly when, but I stopped thinking about things, like what my wife, or my kids, or even my face will look like in a few years."

93

"Don't worry about it, everything's going to be all right."

He didn't really need her to say anything, so he barely heard her at all.

"I don't know how people can stand to see their faces change."

"Well, there's lots of sophisticated techniques that can take care of things like that."

He didn't hear what she said that time, either. He drove and talked. The gun was tucked in his pants, and it felt cold against his stomach. It felt good.

"It's cool. I mean, I'm glad I'm not thinking about my face anymore."

I don't think people should go around wondering what their faces are going to look like a bunch of years from now.

She put her hand over his mouth.

"Everything's fine."

This time he heard her.

"Nothing is fine. But that's the way it goes."

42

It was raining again. It rained so much that it didn't seem like summer anymore. He knew that after the summer rains, it would get hot again, hot enough to go to the sea, and it would stay hot for days, a long long time, long enough to get tired of it. But I think that right then, he forgot everything he knew, he got confused and really thought that the summer was over right then and there.

The car flew down the road, just barely making the curves, and little rivers of rainwater trickled in through the open window, sprinkling his face as if to say—hello, or fuck you.

He was going even faster now. When he looked over at the passenger's seat, he realized he was alone.

43

They showed his picture on TV. It was an old photo, of the two of us together. My grandmother had taken it, and I'd never seen it before. In my family, we never took photos. We didn't like them, not my mother, not my brother, not me. We all agreed on that.

My picture didn't make it on TV. Just his. They cut me out.

He ordered another beer. When he finished it, he ordered another one, and then another one and then another one until he'd had ten. The bar was full, full of mothers and fathers and little kids, all of them in their bathing suits. It was one of those snack bars down by the beach, where you go in, order, and then go outside to a table under the umbrellas.

She was gone. Well, really, he had kicked her out of the car. At the time, she didn't like it one bit, but in the end, I think she probably appreciated it. No matter what she says.

He walked around for a while, up and down the boardwalk that connected all the snack bars along the beach. It was very very hot, but he couldn't go swimming just like that. I think he just couldn't stand the idea of having to walk across the sand, through all those people, to get to the water. And there wasn't any way he could separate himself from his gun.

44

The beach was swarming. Swarming with kids. Swarming with men and women and dogs. Swarming with hats and visors and radios and Walkmans and Discmans and all kinds of waterproof electronic shit, swarming with everything.

Swarming with fear, too.

"He could've killed any one of us, or *all* of us."

When they found out that he'd spent the morning on the beach, everyone went crazy, imagining their faces full of smoke, their kids' faces full of smoke, the faces of their loved ones. Full of smoke.

There were so many of them. But just one of him.

One bullet and a million enemies. If he'd really been

thinking about killing someone, it would have been a tough choice, with all those people on the beach.

When the first helicopter appeared, he knew that everyone there had betrayed him.

45

He stepped off the boardwalk and onto the sand. It wasn't easy, walking in the sand with his boots on, but he never took off his leather boots. The helicopter followed his every move. He just strolled across the beach through the crowds of people, like it was no big deal. He was all in black, and everyone else was almost naked. He was like a twisted black handkerchief in the middle of a smooth, luminous day. Everyone stared at him. Girls called out to him but he didn't see them. Well, maybe he did look at a few of them, or maybe all of them, or maybe he looked at the guys, maybe he was a fag after all. What the fuck does it matter? What does matter is that he walked across the beach to the water and everyone ran away from him as if he were the shadow of the devil.

I told everyone that I hadn't heard from him since he

left our house, but that was a lie. Just before he looked up at the sky and realized that it was all about to end, just before walking across the beach with his pistol and his bullet, he phoned me.

I was alone in the house.

"Hi. It's me. I would've hung up if someone else had answered."

"Thanks."

I don't know why I said that. I don't know why I said any of the things I said, to be honest.

"How's Mother?"

"She's good, I think she's a little crazy right now, but she's fine."

"Good . . . well, I don't really care so much anymore, although sometimes I do. It's almost like she isn't my mother anymore, or maybe having a mother doesn't matter now. I'm pretty much alone now. But I'm okay, I like it this way. I had ten beers already today. So are you reading enough?"

"Yeah, I think so . . . I don't have all that much time these days. The police are always around, and all the television people, reporters . . ."

"How do I look on TV?"

"Cool. Fucking cool. Mother's been going crazy trying to find that video, the one the neighbors made right after they bought that camcorder. But she can't find it."

"Read all the books in my bedroom. Reading is good. Although I don't know exactly what for."

"On TV they never talk about how much you read. I even told them about how you're a poet, but they don't even care."

"I'm not a poet. So don't go around saying bullshit like that. It's one thing to read poetry, but it's a whole other thing to be a poet."

"Well, now you're a murderer."

"Yeah. That's true. What do you think?"

"Well, it's fine with me. But I don't think anyone else would agree. Everyone says that the cops are going to kill you, or else throw you in jail for the rest of your life."

"Well, who knows. It's a nice day out here. The beach is full. This morning I went in the water with my boots on . . . fuck . . . I must be going crazy."

"How are they?"

"My boots? They're okay. How about yours?"

I looked down at them. They were okay too. I hadn't gone in the water with them. I wasn't going crazy.

"Fine."

"So you really don't think it's so bad that I killed those people?"

"No. Really, I don't care. I guess they must've done something to piss you off."

"The security guard at the store, the one that's always there, the one that always fucks with us, he grabbed my arm and called me a thief in front of everyone. I didn't steal a thing."

"They always do that."

"Yeah, but this time I had a gun. He had his and I had mine, so for once, we were playing fair."

"What about the other guy?"

"The one in the gas station? I killed him because of something he said."

"About the girl?"

"Yeah, something really sick. She was asleep in the back-seat and I swear she looked like an angel. Then he came over and said something dirty about her, so that's why I shot him. Right in the face. It's easier to shoot them in the face. Without a face, they're dead, even before the rest of the body goes."

"So what are you going to do now?"

"No idea, man. But I'm not going to jail for the rest of my life. No way."

"So, did you hear about Michael Jackson and Lisa Marie?"

"Yeah. You know, I think that's what I'm going to do. Lie down on the beach and wait for the coming of little Elvis Jackson."

"Listen. I know one of the cops who's on his way to kill you. Actually, he's a pretty good friend of mine. He thinks you seem like a nice guy."

"Cool. How will I know which one is him? I mean, I guess they'll send more than one."

"He looks a lot like Harry Dean Stanton."

"Great. You know, I'm telling you this because I still don't know what it's going to feel like when I'm in front of them and they're ready to kill me. I guess everything will change and I'll really go fucking crazy. I don't understand what's going on, I don't understand it at all. I just don't know what to do when they grab me and tell me I stole something when I didn't steal anything. I never thought I'd find a gun like that in a garbage can, and I never thought that killing people would be so easy."

"That car you've got . . . is it fast?"

"Yeah. But not fast enough."

We were silent for a while. I didn't know what to say and I figured he must've had a thousand things on his mind. Maybe we both just had less and less to think about. I don't know. There's no way to know for sure.

"Listen, shrimp, I'm running out of change . . . be good. Read a lot, and polish your boots and don't think that everything I did was bad . . ."

"Okay."

"But don't think that everything I did was good, either . . . Maybe it was just a new and more spectacular way to fuck things up."

"Where are you going now?"

"To the water. You know what James Joyce said? That a pier is a frustrated bridge."

He hung up first and then I did. I never told anyone about this phone call.

Until now.

46

"I got him in the arm. I was aiming for his legs but I got him in the arm instead. I've got a lousy aim."

My friend, the cop, ordered us some drinks. At first the waiter said something about my being underage, but when he saw the police badge, he shut up, and from then on treated me like I was a sumo wrestler or something.

We were drinking whisky. He took it straight, and I put a piece of ice in mine. We both smoked nonstop.

"Then I got him in the chest. I didn't want to aim that high, I was afraid of ruining his face. He was so goddamned good-looking. That would have been enough, but the men behind me went insane. Shot him up like maniacs, I'm telling you, it was a fucking war. I never saw anything like it—the SWAT team, the secret police, the local cops, there were guys shooting from everywhere—even from the fucking helicopter. They ripped him apart. Fucking scumbags, fifty hungry sons of bitches firing at one dead duck. When they finally stopped, I went over to the body, but it wasn't your brother anymore. There was a kid lying on the ground. But it didn't look a thing like him."

We each took another gulp of whisky. You'd think my throat would be burning up, but it wasn't. The truth is it went down like water. Much better than water.

"What did you play?"

I was silent. I didn't really know what he meant.

"When you were kids? What kind of games did you play?"

"Bruce Lee."

"Fuck, you're kidding—I love Bruce Lee."

He got up and started making these karate moves.

"HIIIAAAAAAAAA! HAIIIIIIIO!"

He waved his hands and legs around. He made a lot of noise, but he didn't really know what he was doing.

Everyone in the bar was looking at him, the waiters and everything, but he had already shown them his badge.

"Bruce Lee, fucking wild . . . You know, when he died, Steve McQueen and James Coburn carried his coffin. Shit. Steve McQueen."

He finished his drink in one gulp, and I did the same. The waiter came back over.

He ordered two more whiskies.

"Your brother's the second person I've killed. He was the better of the two, by far. You know, in the middle of all that shit . . . maybe I shouldn't say it . . . what the fuck, you're not going to say anything . . . listen, can you keep a secret?"

I said of course. There's not too many things I can do, but I can keep a secret. That's for sure.

"In the middle of all that shit, with all those fuckers ripping that poor kid apart, I started firing my gun at everything. It was all pretty fucked up, I mean nothing about it was normal, everyone was going nuts . . . so I pointed my gun away from him and at my men. I only got one of them, in the leg. I don't think they'll get me on it. I was aiming for his head, or maybe I was shooting with my eyes closed, I don't know . . . I don't remember, all I know is that I didn't want your brother to kill me and I was scared shitless, and all that noise was driving me fucking insane."

I motioned to the waiter and he brought over two more whiskies. We still hadn't finished the ones we already had, but I didn't know what else I was supposed to be doing.

"The motherfuckers actually lined themselves up to shoot him. Just so they could say they did it. They all wanted to be fucking stars, but I'm telling you it was me who shot him. By the time those assholes opened fire he was already dead . . . well, practically."

We both ignored the half-filled glasses and drank from the new ones. I was trying to keep up with him, but it wasn't so easy.

"You want to do a line?"

He slid his hand over the table, like he was giving me something invisible. I took the envelope and I went down to the bathroom.

I went into a stall, and opened the envelope. It took me a while, and a bunch of the stuff sprinkled onto the floor. I tried to pick it up, but then I stopped. I did one line, and then a little bit more. I used a rolled-up bill. Just like in the movies.

When I left the bathroom I felt great.

I gave him back the envelope and then he went down. He was in there a while before he came back.

When he sat down again, he took a gulp of his whisky.

"Fuck, God only knows what he was thinking about then. He didn't even have any bullets left . . . You know, I almost killed a dog once? He was sick and my wife thought that it would be real easy for me to do. So that it wouldn't suffer any more. That's what she said. But we all suffer, kid, all of us . . ."

He paused for a second, and I felt like I should say something.

"Yes sir, all of us."

"So I grabbed the gun and put it behind the dog's ear, and he looked at me out of the corner of his eye. Shit, it was my own dog, but even if it hadn't been, I still couldn't have done it. There's no way you can kill a dog. Your brother fired his last bullet into the air. I don't know why. He could've shot me, or anyone else, but he fired straight up into thin air. I didn't aim at the air, I aimed at his leg. But I got him in the arm. I've got a lousy aim."

We finished our drinks and went home. I mean, I went to my house. I don't know where he went.

I felt okay, but after a while I felt worse than I had before. It was as if someone had given me something and then taken it right back.

47

We should've been able to see it on TV, but the police kept the reporters and all their cameras as far away from the beach as possible. The last picture they showed was a long shot from the boardwalk with people running in every direction, screaming their heads off. He headed for the water while everyone else ran in the opposite direction, scared to death, just like in the movie *Jaws.* Some people were injured, although they exaggerated that, too.

People just stood there watching from the boardwalk, like it was a big circus. Dozens of ambulances and fire trucks and about a million squad cars came in after him. As they took away the wounded, people shouted and clapped their hands. He didn't have anywhere else to go. There he was, in the water again, with his boots on.

One helicopter landed on the beach and another hovered up above, right overhead, like a shrewd insect. The squad cars were arranged in a semicircle around the scene.

One of the cops started shouting at him. It was very very

hot. He shouted for a while until my brother raised his gun. Then the cop stopped shouting and for a second, it was totally silent. Then he shot his last bullet straight up into the air, as if he were starting a race.

48

He was on the front page of the newspaper, in a photo taken from one of the SWAT team's helicopters. It was almost impossible to make him out, all you could see was a tiny black figure surrounded by a bunch of yellow umbrellas. The police were in the picture, under the umbrellas. Further in the background, you could see the reporters and even further, all the courageous sunbathers and their equally courageous families.

The canaries finally cornered the cat.

49

When he kicked her out of the car, it was already parked on the side of the road. She swore that the car was still moving, but I know that he never would've done something like that. He didn't say anything to her before he did it and he didn't say anything to her afterward. He just stopped in the middle of the road and pushed her out of the car. When she realized what had happened, he was already gone.

"We spent the morning by the sea. It was early, and nobody else was around, so we ate and drank beer, and he seemed pretty happy. He laughed a little. He even went into the water, with all his clothes on. I took mine off. I have a really good body. Small tits, but that was the way he liked them."

She lifted up her blouse and showed them to me. Beautiful tits. Beautiful girl.

"He was so good-looking, but so weird. So now everyone's writing me letters, I don't know what to do with them all. At least my father doesn't hit me anymore. He really beat me up when I first went back, but when they started showing me on TV, he got scared. He knew that if he kept it up, I'd tell the whole world on TV, so now he doesn't touch me. I'm a star now and nobody touches a star unless she tells them to. So . . . do you answer any of the letters that you get?"

"Some of them, the ones that are addressed to me. But not all of those, even. Most of the people who write them are lunatics. Some are okay. But not many."

"I get the same thing. Almost all of them are from girls who want to know what kind of shampoo I use or if I'm a natural redhead or if I can help them get started as models. By the way, I've already got an agent. They took a bunch of pictures of me and said that they can send me on assignment in Japan. Except I don't know if I really want to go to Japan. I also got an offer to do a TV show. A talk show."

She was pretty excited about things. She didn't seem too bothered that my brother was dead.

"He shouldn't have thrown me out of the car."

"He did it for your sake, don't you get it? If he hadn't kicked you out, you'd be six feet under right now. No agent. No Japan. No nothing."

She didn't get mad when I said that. She never got mad. She just glided over unpleasant things, like a skater glides over ice.

"I don't know about that . . . If I'd stayed, maybe he'd be alive right now, and maybe we'd be on our way to Japan, you know, together."

Maybe she forgot about the two people he'd killed, one of them right in front of her.

"I know what you're thinking, but it's not like that . . .

He wouldn't have stayed in jail for all that long. He was famous."

We were out having dinner together, but she was the
only one eating. I drank so many beers that by the end of
the night, I didn't know what the hell we were both talking
about.

"They say they love this type of stuff in Japan. I mean,
I'd never kill anyone, obviously, but they don't know that.
They see me as one of those deadly teenagers. You can make
a lot of money off something like this. Not that I care that
much about money, but I like to travel, and anyway, I want
to get as far away as possible from that psycho father of mine
and his fucking fists and my mother's pathetic face and the
fucking miserable life I had before he came along and
plucked me out of there, like a healthy tooth out of a rotten
mouth."

"You've got a ton of letters there."

She hauled out a plastic bag and dumped it on the table.
Hundreds of letters. I had a lot of plastic bags like that, too.
I guess there are a lot of people in this world who would
rather talk to a stranger or even a ghost than to nobody at
all. She sure talked to me.

"Are you going to a psychiatrist?"

"Yeah, I started a couple of weeks ago, but I didn't talk
much, so they let me take a break for a while. I'll start up
again in a few weeks. They said if I didn't like this guy they'd
find me another one."

"That's the same thing they said to me, but I'm still with
the same one. I asked them for another one, for a girl, a lady.
I mean, because there are some things I just can't say to a
man with a beard."

"He's got a beard?"

"Ugh, a huge one, he's like a bear. Like a big scraggly bear."

I don't know why, but I started thinking that maybe if my shrink had a beard, things might be a lot better.

I picked out a letter from her pile, like the way they do on those TV contests.

The guy who wrote this one was a pig. He tried to make it seem like he was a kid, but you just knew he was at least fifty.

"This is disgusting. Do you get a lot like this?"

"Some, yeah. One even sent me a picture of his dick. I threw it out. Anyway, it wasn't such a big dick."

I ordered another beer. I didn't like her talking like that, because she really was much better than that.

"Listen. You shouldn't let anyone talk like that to you, or touch you or anything. Get yourself away from all those pigs. Get away from their pig knuckles and pig snouts and pig fantasies and especially their big disgusting dicks."

I think I was pretty drunk by then.

"Go to Japan, will you, and never come back. The Japanese are respectable people and they don't know at all. The less people know about you, the less they can hurt you. So go to Japan, and take all your goddamned letters with you."

I started to cry, but then right away I stopped. I hadn't cried since I was nine. She was scared but intrigued. She was so incredibly gorgeous and she'd even shown me her little tits right in the middle of that empty restaurant and I was drunk and I was crying and I was still a virgin and my brother was a murderer and a dead murderer on top of it, and all of this put together was getting to be just a little too much for me.

"Are you okay?"

"No, I'm not, and I'll never go to Japan and I'm never going anywhere."

She patted me on the head, as if I were a little kid, or a dog.

"Don't say things like that. Anyone can go to Japan nowadays, it's not that far away."

I finished my beer and left. I didn't even say good-bye. I just walked out of there, standing up tall, straight as a board.

If it wasn't so far away, then I didn't want to go there.

all the planes in the world

50

On one of his tapes, he'd recorded the voice of a madman. The words of a madman.

> *"Stop following me . . . I don't know where I'm go-*
> *ing . . . Stop looking at me . . . Stop following me . . .*
> *Stop listening to me—go to hell, all of you! . . . My*
> *mother can't touch me anymore . . . My father can't*
> *touch me, either . . . I can't touch anything . . . It's*
> *all scattered . . . It's all free . . . It's all alone . . . No-*
> *body can count on anyone . . . Better, better, better . . .*
> *God doesn't know what the hell he's in for . . . God*
> *is a scared little girl . . . God doesn't have no bicy-*
> *cle . . . God's got no dick . . . God's jealous . . . God*
> *lives in Hawaii . . . God plays ukelele . . . God don't*
> *know where the hell he's going."*

After that, there was noise, somebody was honking a horn for almost ten minutes. Probably one of those guys stuck in his car, with another guy double-parked next to him.

Then there were two kids talking, in a park, I think, because you could hear other kids talking and playing.

"I'm not always going to be here, you know . . ."
"I could knock you down . . ."
"It doesn't matter, it's not like I'm always going to be here."

51

"My God, I've never seen such huge airplanes."

The airplanes were taking off and landing just behind them. They were so close that it seemed like you could just jump onto one of them and take off, anywhere.

"I wonder where they're going."

She looked up at the planes. She pointed at them, and followed them with her finger.

"Look at them go . . . look at them . . . where are they all going?"

"To Russia, to China, all over."

"To Cuba?"

"Yeah, Cuba too."

"But nobody wants to go to Cuba. People are trying to escape from Cuba. They paddle their way out of there in fucking soup cans."

"That's all propaganda; besides, there's always someone who wants to go where everyone else is escaping from."

"What for?"

"I don't know. To piss people off, I guess."

A plane swooped past him. Big, as a big house. Close, too. So close a jump would get you on.

"If you could go anywhere, where would you go?"

"Australia."

"Australia, what's in Australia? There's nothing good in Australia."

"It doesn't have to be any good; as long as it's on the other side."

A huge plane cut through the sky and descended, until it smashed against the ground, softly. More planes passed, without messing his hair up or anything. It was nighttime now, and then it would turn into day and all the planes in the world would continue passing through that very same spot.